Table Manners

P9-CAB-546
3 1965 00111 7396

JAN 1 8 2002

Alexandra

Friend of yours

Corin

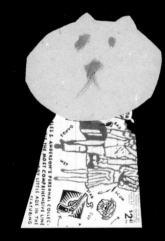

Your dog or cat

Sasha

Ingo

Kolia

Anya

Maddy

E
RAD Palos Heights Public Library
12501 S. 71st Avenue
Palos Heights, IL 60463

What you need is...

Table

Thanks to Paul Colin—a virtuoso. Clean hands! Spotless screen!

Copyright © 2001 by Chris Raschka and Vladimir Radunsky

All rights reserved. No part of this book may be reproduced, transmitted, or stored in an information retrieval system in any form or by any means, graphic, electronic, or mechanical, including photocopying, taping, and recording, without prior written permission from the publisher.

First edition 2001

Library of Congress Cataloging-in-Publication Data is available.

Library of Congress Catalog Card Number 2001025145

ISBN 0-7636-1453-X

10 9 8 7 6 5 4 3 2 1

Printed in Italy

This book was typeset in Univers.

The illustrations were done in mixed media.

visit us at www.candlewick.com

Candlewick Press

2067 Massachusetts Avenue • Cambridge, Massachusetts 02140

Manners

the edifying story of two friends whose discovery of good manners promises them a glorious future

Chris Raschka

Vladimir Radunsky

Listen to me carefully, Dudunya.

a spoon,

a fork,

a plate,

it's very, very important,

To begin with, you need:

a **knife,**

 a **glass,**

it's very important,

and a **napkin,**

it's very, very, very important.

But why?

Because:

eating without a plate

Filthy

Leopard style

Zebra style

But Chester,

Because it makes you look grown-up,

REALLY nICE-Looking gROWN-uP DudunyA

drinking without a glass

dining without a napkin

filthy ugly

ugly

Wild BOAR style

* please do not confuse horrible wild boar with a pig; a wild boar is far more disgusting than a pig.

why a fork and a knife?

and because a knife makes big things small enough to fit into your mouth.

Big Potato

16-Bite Potato-Eating Method

Chester, Look! I'm using my napkin.

Well done, Dudunya!
Just one thing: napkins are for wiping your mouth.

Napkins are definitely not

crowns

flags

mops

whips

handkerchiefs

scarves

parachutes

masks

everything that is not a napkin

A real story told to *Dudunya by his friend Alexander about a man who didn't know about napkins.*

Once there was   a man who wiped his mouth with his hands and then wiped his hands on his pants. One day he was told that this was bad manners. So now he always bends far enough over to wipe his mouth right on his pants. Oh, poor, poor man.

Good Lord! The Queen is coming for breakfast! How will you fold the napkins?

1.
Lay the napkin flat.
Be careful.

2.
Tie a lovely little knot in one of the corners.

3.

Gently repeat this on the other three corners.

Only the Queen may wear her napkin as a crown!

Great Scott! The President is coming for dinner! Make ready the napkins!

Lay the napkin flat.

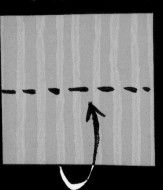

Fold your napkin in half! From the bottom to the top.

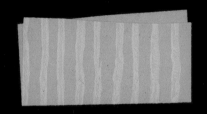

Only the President may wave his napkin like a flag!

Dudunya, I beg you, listen

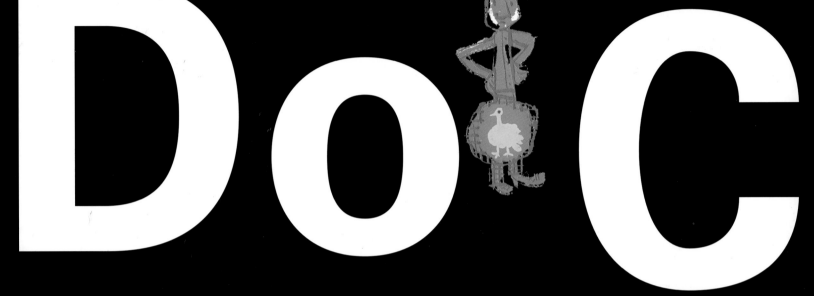

Do C

See what happens when you don't?

Fresh Watermelon

Catch of the Day

to your Chester.

hew

Beef Wellington

Dudunya, darling.

Never speak with your mouth full.
It's very, very, very important. This
I learned from my father's father's
father. One day you will pass this
on to your children's children's
children.

Palos Heights Public Library
12501 S. 71st Avenue
Palos Heights, IL 60463

Full-Mouthed Speaking Accidents

1. chocolate-covered Father

2. mother with sprinkles

3. Breaded Brother.

4. Glazed Sister

5. Candied Dog

6. Shawarma Uncle

7.

8. Cousin in Cream Sauce

9.

Palos Heights Public Library
12501 S. 71st Avenue
Palos Heights, IL 60463

When? What?

What do we eat first when we get up? Toothpaste? Dessert?

Good heavens, no, Dudunya. We eat breakfast.

When do I have lunch? At noon, my dear. And if you need a little something between breakfast and lunch, you have elevenses. *When do I have elevenses?* At eleven, my friend. *I like that. I like that very, very much.* What do you have when you come home from school?

I don't know, Chester. What? A snack. Crackers and juice and fruit and something nice and something delicious. *What am I eating after snack?* Nothing. *Oh, no. Chester, please, I'll be hungry again.*

Good news, Dudunya—dinner is served at six o'clock.

What about dessert?

I know.

I don't know.

No dessert till after you

Make your selection for tomorrow's dessert:

☐ **chocolate chocolate chocolate**

☐ **Gummi Bear pie**

Dudunya, look, I'm a *Virtuoso*

Don't try this at home.

Clean shirt!

Are you ready to eat at the Queen's palace?

not ready

Eater

Clean hands!

Are you ready to dine with the President?

ready

Boys! Girls!

Good table manners will take you around the world.

Breakfast in France	*S'il vous plaît*
Elevenses in England	*Please*
Lunch in Italy	*Per favore*
Snack in Brazil	*Por favor*
Dinner in China	*Ching*
Milk in Russia	*Pojaluista*

Impress your hosts wherever you go and make them invite you back. Just say this:

Merci

Thank you

Grazie

Obrigado

Shieh shieh

Spasibo

The Final Exam

1. A girl, **Mimsy**, is lying on the floor in the restaurant. She should

 a. stay there and roar like a tiger.

 b. be quiet and try to sleep.

 c. eat what she finds on the floor.

 d. go back to her seat with a nice smile.

2. A boy, **Chip**, is trying to play tag with a waiter. He should

 a. run faster and jump on him.

 b. hide under a table and then jump on him.

 c. ask more children to join the game, too.

 d. go back to his seat with a nice smile.

3. A girl, **Binky**, is sniffing around other people's tables looking at what they are eating and listening to their conversations. She should

 a. join in their conversations.

 b. taste some food on their plates.

 c. approach quietly, ignore their conversation, pay no attention to the food on their plates, but try to taste their dessert.

 d. go back to her seat with a nice smile.

4. A waiter is asking a boy, **Skipper**, what he wants to order. He should

 a. immediately hide under the table.

 b. refuse to answer, and say, "You'll never get it out of me."

 c. make his choice and speak up.

 d. stay in his seat with a nice smile.

(in the restaurant)

sniffing **Binky**

a zipped **Skipper**

mighty **Mimsy**

a waiter chasing **Chip**

Look

at me, Chester,

I'm irresistibly clean.
I will never eat again.

Oh, no,
Dudunya, no.
You have
to eat
to live.

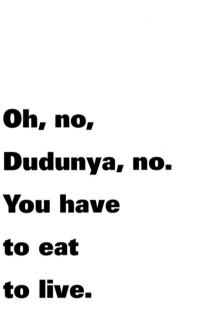

Just remember
your table manners!

Corin

You

Your dog or cat

Ingo

Anna

Maddy

Alexandra

Nicholas

Friend of yours